ROBOT-BOT-BOT

Also by Fernando Krahn

Catch That Cat!
The Mystery of the Giant Footprints
Who's Seen the Scissors?
April Fools
A Flying Saucer Full of Spaghetti
Gustavus and Stop

ROBOT-BOT-BOT

Fernando Krahn

E. P. DUTTON   NEW YORK

Library of Congress Cataloging in Publication Data

Krahn, Fernando.   Robot-bot-bot.
SUMMARY: A family's new robot is all work and no play
until the daughter takes matters into her own hands.
[1. Robots—Fiction.   2. Stories without words]   I. Title.
PZ7.K8585Ro   1979   [E]   78-21959   ISBN: 0-525-38545-2

Published in the United States by E. P. Dutton, a Division
of Sequoia-Elsevier Publishing Company, Inc., New York

Published simultaneously in Canada by Clarke,
Irwin & Company Limited, Toronto and Vancouver

Editor: Ann Troy   Designer: Stacie Rogoff
Printed in the U.S.A.   First Edition   10 9 8 7 6 5 4 3 2 1

FERNANDO KRAHN was born and educated in Chile. For several years he worked as a cartoonist in New York. Now he, his wife María Luz, and their three children live near Barcelona, Spain.

Mr. Krahn has created a number of other popular wordless books, including *Catch That Cat!*, *The Mystery of the Giant Footprints*, and *April Fools*. In addition, he and his wife have collaborated on several books, and he has also illustrated the work of other children's book writers.